ideals

50th
ANNIVERSARY
COLLECTOR'S EDITION

ideals

Christmas

COVER OF PREMIER ISSUE
IDEALS CHRISTMAS 1944

Published by Ideals Publications Incorporated, 565 Marriott Drive, Nashville, Tennessee 37214

Copyright © 1994 by Ideals Publications Incorporated
Printed and bound in the U.S.A.

ISBN 0-8249-1126-1

IDEALS PUBLICATIONS INCORPORATED
NASHVILLE, TENNESSEE

FIFTY YEARS AGO

Ideals magazine began more than fifty years ago in Milwaukee, Wisconsin, when Van B. Hooper, a public relations manager for a local manufacturer, began adding poetry and homey philosophy to the company newsletter. Employee response was enthusiastic; before long workers were sharing Mr. Hooper's newsletter with friends and family members, who found expression for their own values in the words and pictures chosen by Mr. Hooper. By the early forties, Mr. Hooper was mailing his newsletter to readers throughout the Milwaukee area and beyond.

In 1944 Mr. Hooper decided to turn his newsletter into a magazine, with each and every page devoted to the kind of uplifting poetry and stories that had been heretofore squeezed in between items of company news. He chose the name *Ideals* for his fledgling magazine and, in September of 1944, went to press with the very first Christmas issue, little expecting that fifty years later his simple magazine would be an American institution.

In the early years, the magazine earned new subscribers through word of mouth alone; Americans, apparently, were eager for the kind of old-fashioned, homespun values that Mr. Hooper's magazine espoused. *Ideals* grew with every year, eventually expanding to eight issues a year mailed throughout the United States and Canada. The magazine remained a Hooper family venture for almost thirty-five years until, in 1977, Mr. Hooper's heir sold the company to a larger publishing company. The foundation laid by Van Hooper was a strong one, however, and the tradition of *Ideals* was well-respected by the new publishers. Today the magazine, again privately owned, is published in Nashville, Tennessee, far away from its Milwaukee roots but still little removed from the values behind Mr. Hooper's first newsletters. Fifty years old this year, *Ideals* is still treasured by American families who believe that no matter how times change, the simple things—family ties, love of country, and faith in God—are what see us through.

In this anniversary issue of *Ideals* we celebrate the fiftieth year of our magazine with a collection of text from the magazines of the forties, along with artwork and photos from the first decades. We invite you to look back with us through the years. Each poem, story, quotation is exactly as it appeared fifty years ago, and although you may laugh at a phrase or marvel at how times have changed, we believe you will also find that the words that inspired, amused, and comforted *Ideals* readers fifty years ago more often than not do the same today.

THE IDEALS OF CHRISTMAS

Drawing by George Hinke, IDEALS CHRISTMAS 1955
Painting opposite by George Hinke, IDEALS CHRISTMAS 1950

Christmas was simpler in 1944. The very first issue of *Ideals* magazine—*Christmas* 1944—reflected the values of the times; its pages were full of poems, stories, artwork, and photography celebrating family, tradition, and the miracle of Jesus' birth. In 1944, before the Christmas season began in October, before so many people counted shopping days more carefully than the days of Advent, American families embraced *Ideals* as part of their Christmas tradition. Fifty years later, *Ideals Christmas* remains a cherished annual reminder of the simpler, more magical days of a fun, old-fashioned family Christmas.

DEAR SANTA

Signs of Christmas

Edgar A. Guest

IDEALS CHRISTMAS 1948
Drawing by John Walter, IDEALS CHRISTMAS 1965

When a pair of little nippers
Ask if they can get your slippers
Or put up a furious battle
To be first upon your knee,
When with loving care they task you,
As their grandpa, let me ask you:
Do you need someone to tell you
Just what day is soon to be?

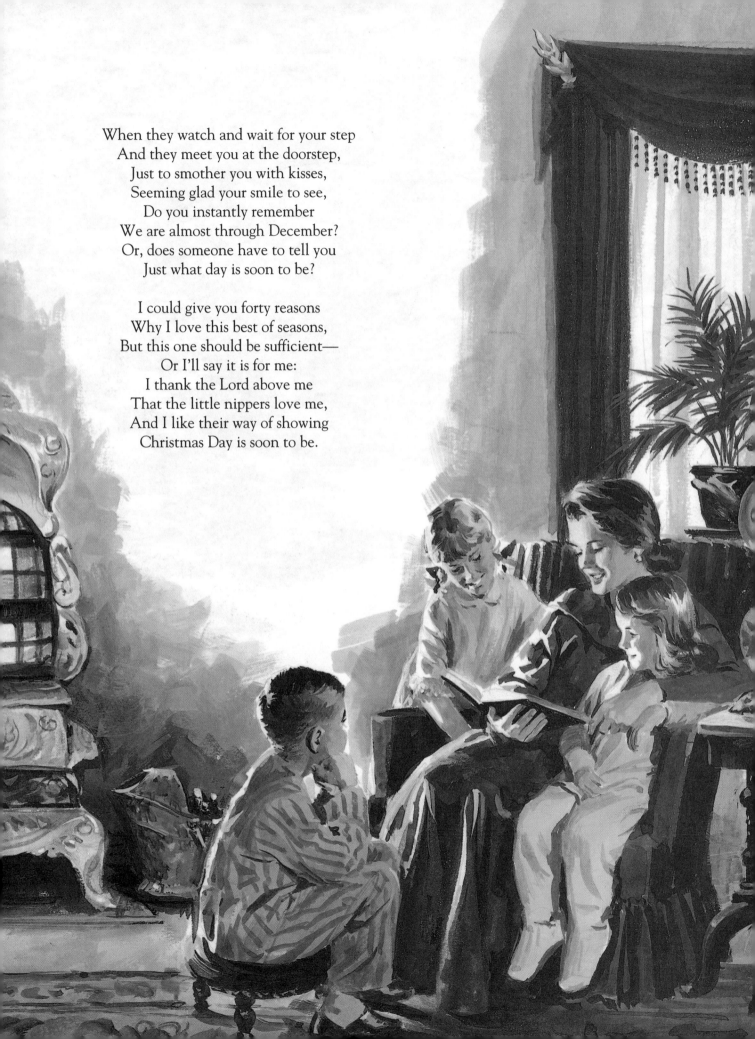

When they watch and wait for your step
And they meet you at the doorstep,
Just to smother you with kisses,
Seeming glad your smile to see,
Do you instantly remember
We are almost through December?
Or, does someone have to tell you
Just what day is soon to be?

I could give you forty reasons
Why I love this best of seasons,
But this one should be sufficient—
Or I'll say it is for me:
I thank the Lord above me
That the little nippers love me,
And I like their way of showing
Christmas Day is soon to be.

Dear Santa-

The thing I want the most
Is just a little pup,
I'll take just any kind you have,
Tiny, middle-sized or up.

Santa, it seems my heart is lonely,
Just any dog will do,
So long as he will romp and play,
To me, he will be new.

Santa, do dogs grow in your cold North?
Dogs, for lonely boys,
I have so many, many things,
In the way of books and toys

Santa, my little playmates down the street,
Own a cat, a bird, one has a frog,
But Santa, I'll be satisfied
If you'll just bring me a dog.

Drawing by Cliff Sutherland, IDEALS CHRISTMAS 1964.

Sleigh Bells

Edgar A. Guest

IDEALS CHRISTMAS 1948
Photograph opposite by Ralph Luedtke, IDEALS CHRISTMAS 1967

In forty years we've changed the world and traded many things:
We've banished glowing stoves to gain the warmth a furnace brings;
We've polished off discomforts with invention's magic art;
We've built the "press-the-button" age when countless motors start.
But thinking of my boyhood days, we lost a joy, I'll say,
When faithful horse and cutter were forever put away.
For never comes a fall of snow but what for them I mourn,
And that strap of tinkling sleigh bells we supplanted with a horn!

I would not now go back to live as once we lived of old;
I'm much too fond of comfort to undress in bedrooms cold.
On winter nights I would not care to journey to the shed
And carry coal to feed the stove before I go to bed.
I'm glad such chores exist no more, and I am grateful, too,
That wheeling out the ashes is a task with which I'm through.

I'm not the kind that loves the past and all that's modern scorns;
I merely say that sleigh bells were more musical than horns.
We give up youth for mellow age; each forward step we take
To reach a joy which lies ahead, an old charm we forsake.
We deal and barter through the years old customs for the new,
Find easier ways to do the tasks once difficult to do.
But sometimes as we move along to build the better day,
We learn we've been compelled to throw a lovely thing away.
And thinking of my boyhood days, to this I will be sworn:
Those sleigh bells sang a prettier song than any motor horn.

THE SLEIGH RACE.

Christmas Days of Long Ago

Frank Carleton Nelson

IDEALS CHRISTMAS 1948
Drawing by Donald Mills, IDEALS CHRISTMAS 1967
Overleaf: Santa on the Housetop by George Hinke
Cover, IDEALS CHRISTMAS 1946

I'd love to take a journey back
Through time and feel the joy
That oft was mine in other years,
When I was just a boy.
I'd love to know the pleasures now
That then were mine to know,
The thrills that came on Christmas Day
In years of long ago.

The world today may look the same,
As far as looks may go,
The trees the same as trees looked then,
And just the same the snow.
The songs we sing are just the same,
And recitations, too;
In fact we're doing many things
The way we used to do.

The roads are paved and better now
Than in the days of yore.
A thousand comforts now are ours
We never knew before.
The sights are fine on Christmas Day,
I really must admit;
And yet, somehow, it seems to me
There's something wrong with it.

I'd love to ride the old bobsled,
And hear the horses neigh,
And hear the jingle of the bells
That seemed to make the day.
I'd love to journey back once more
And live it o'er again;
I'd love to see a Christmas now
Just like I saw it then.

But styles have changed, and ways have changed,
And time has taken toll;
Yet memories sweet of other days
Are written on the soul.
And while today I live them o'er
With children by the tree,
I feel a longing in my heart
For those that used to be.

The Chimes of Christmas Eve

Pliny A. Wiley

IDEALS CHRISTMAS 1948
Photograph by Ralph Luedtke
Painting opposite by George Hinke, IDEALS CHRISTMAS 1967

The chimes ring out on Christmas Eve
So sweet and clear across the snow;
In mystic music they retrieve
The memories fond of long ago.

They chime of hallowed Bethlehem,
When angel heralds of the King
Sang peace, while from Jerusalem
The star-led Wise Men tributes bring.

They chime of saintly souls of old,
Who cherished truth o'er all beside,
Disdaining pleasure, ease and gold,
For Christ they lived; for Him they died.

They chime of childhood's long past day,
A picture hung on memory's walls,
All glorious in its bright array,
A picture that the youth enthralls.

They chime of Christmas Eves to be,
When, borne on wings of angel song,
Goodwill and peace shall make men free,
And right shall rise supreme o'er wrong.

GLORY to God in the highest and on earth Peace Good Will toward men.

Luke 2:14

Calligraphy by Cliff Sutherland, IDEALS CHRISTMAS 1959
Pastel opposite by Cliff Sutherland, IDEALS CHRISTMAS 1948

Let Us Keep Christmas

Grace Noll Crowell

IDEALS CHRISTMAS 1944
Drawing by John Walter, IDEALS CHRISTMAS 1964

Whatever else be lost among the years,
Let us keep Christmas still a shining thing:
Whatever doubts assail us, or what fears,
Let us hold close one day, remembering
Its poignant meaning for the hearts of men.
Let us get back our childlike faith again.

Wealth may have taken wings, yet still there are
Clear windowpanes to glow with candlelight;
There are boughs for garlands and a tinsel star
To tip some little fir tree's lifted height.
There is no heart too heavy or too sad,
But some small gift of love can make it glad.

And there are home-sweet rooms where laughter rings,
And we can sing the carols as of old.
Above the eastern hills a white star swings;
There is an ancient story to be told;
There are kind words and cheering words to say.
Let us be happy on the Christ Child's day.

THE IDEALS OF PATRIOTISM

Drawing by Ray App, *IDEALS HERITAGE* 1973
Painting opposite by George Hinke
Cover, *IDEALS LIBERTY* 1946

Patriotic feelings run high in times of war, and in early 1945, when the second issue of *Ideals—Ideals Patriotic*—appeared, Americans were full to bursting with patriotic pride. The title page of the magazine reminded readers of the sacrifices they were making for the war effort: "Circulation of initial volumes will be very limited," ran a small note above the copyright line, "due to present government restrictions on paper." But Americans were ready and willing to deal with restrictions, shortages, and rationing; for as much as we lamented the tragedy of war, we bravely and gladly accepted the responsibility of our nation to restore and preserve peace in the world. On the pages of *Patriotic Ideals*—and on the pages of countless future issues—are words and pictures that eloquently express the fierce and abiding love of country that binds us together as a nation.

Your Flag and My Flag

Wilbur D. Nesbit

IDEALS PATRIOTIC 1945
Drawing by Donald Mills, IDEALS RURAL 1966

Your flag and my flag,
And how it flies today
In your land and my land
And half a world away!
Rose-red and blood-red
The stripes forever gleam;

Snow-white and soul white—
The good forefathers' dream;
Sky-blue and true blue
With stars to gleam aright—
The gloried guidon of the day,
A shelter through the night.

Your flag and my flag!
To every star and stripe
The drums beat as hearts beat
And fifers shrilly pipe!

Your flag and my flag—
A blessing in the sky;
Your hope and my hope—
It never hid a lie!
Home land and far land
And half the world around,
Old Glory hears our glad salute
And ripples to the sound.

Your flag and my flag!
And, oh, how much it holds—
Your land and my land—
Secure within its folds!

Your heart and my heart
Beat quicker at the sight;
Sun-kissed and wind-tossed—
Red and blue and white.
The one flag, the great flag—
The flag for me and you—
Glorified all else beside—
The red and white and blue.

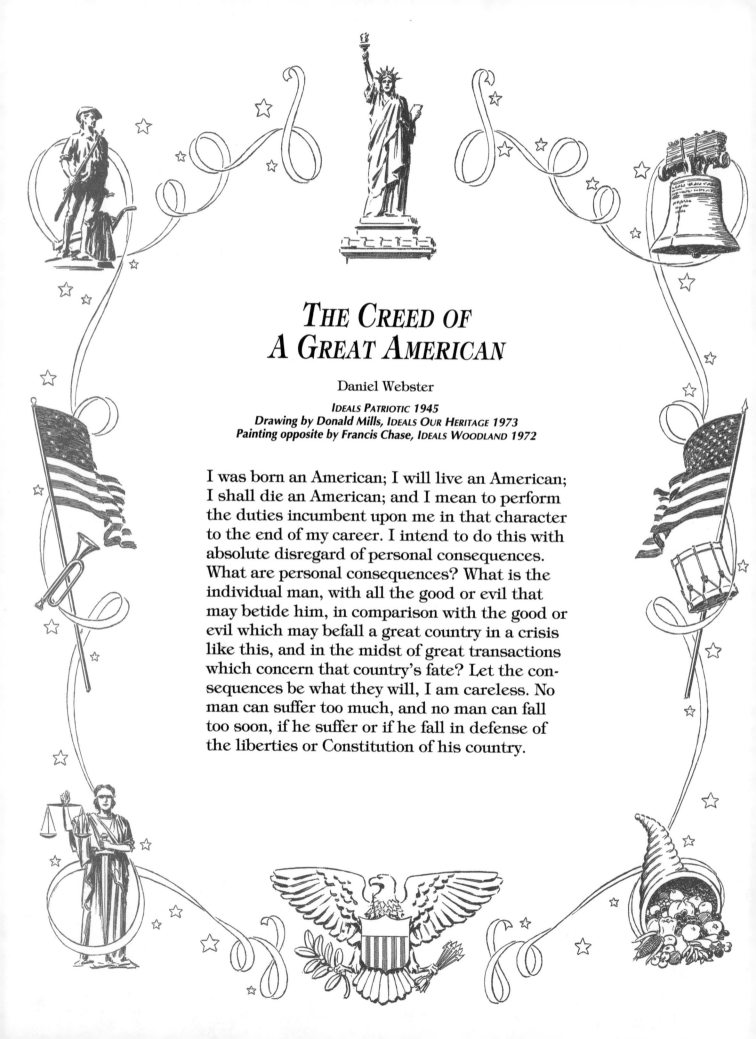

THE CREED OF
A GREAT AMERICAN

Daniel Webster

IDEALS PATRIOTIC 1945
Drawing by Donald Mills, IDEALS OUR HERITAGE 1973
Painting opposite by Francis Chase, IDEALS WOODLAND 1972

I was born an American; I will live an American;
I shall die an American; and I mean to perform
the duties incumbent upon me in that character
to the end of my career. I intend to do this with
absolute disregard of personal consequences.
What are personal consequences? What is the
individual man, with all the good or evil that
may betide him, in comparison with the good or
evil which may befall a great country in a crisis
like this, and in the midst of great transactions
which concern that country's fate? Let the consequences be what they will, I am careless. No
man can suffer too much, and no man can fall
too soon, if he suffer or if he fall in defense of
the liberties or Constitution of his country.

A Mother to Her Son in Service

Grace Noll Crowell

IDEALS PATRIOTIC 1945
Drawing by Ray App, IDEALS VACATION 1968
Photograph opposite by Ralph Luedtke

Wherever you are this day, my precious son,
God hold you close, God keep you safe from harm.
In this strange victory that must be won
It takes your youth, your strength of heart and mind,
Your valor and your courage and your might
To bring to pass the miracle of peace.
God keep you facing forward toward the light
That waits ahead for you when war shall cease.

Take God as your companion, O dear Heart;
We must not, dare not face the days alone.
With Him for comrade we can do our part
And staunchly, bravely face the great unknown.
I, too, must be a valiant soldier, for
That is what mothers are when there is war.

Victory cannot be bought with any amount of money, however large; victory is achieved by the blood of soldiers, the sweat of working men and women, and the sacrifices of all people.

Franklin D. Roosevelt

The success of our republic depends on the fact that we do not suppress, but listen with tolerance to those who express an opposing idea.

Forrest J. Hall

We must be willing to pay a price for freedom, for no price that is ever asked for it is half the cost of doing without it.

H. L. Mencken

My concern is not whether God is on our side; my great concern is to be on God's side.

Abraham Lincoln

Wherever the American flag has gone it has been a herald of a better day—it has been the pledge of freedom, of justice, of order, and of civilization.

A. P. Putman

Our reliance is in the love of liberty which God has planted in us. Our defense is in the spirit which prized liberty as the heritage of all men, in all lands, everywhere.

Abraham Lincoln

No arms will conquer, no battles will be won, unless we make the heart of the struggle loyalty to the values for which Jesus stood.

Rev. Otis R. Rice

Let each and every one of us remember that liberty is a gift not lightly given; that we, within ourselves, must preserve for generations yet unborn a vision of brotherhood among men, until one day all the world shall be ready to share it.

Frederick S. Wilson

In a troubled world he retains his freedom. He can own property, send his children to school, worship as he chooses, express his opinions, get his news through a free press and radio. He is an American.

Henry M. Reed

Drawing by Donald Mills, IDEALS COUNTRY 1967

There is a legend told of a boy who came to a capital where men from all countries were met to talk about life and living. And he turned to an old man to ask, "How can I tell which is an American and which a European, since all are speaking one language?" The old man pondered a moment, and in time he began to speak. And he was heard to say . . .

Thank God for America
Author Unknown

IDEALS PATRIOTIC 1945
Drawing by M. Nye,
IDEALS COUNTRYSIDE 1971
Painting opposite by George Hinke,
IDEALS HISTORIC 1947

Look around you carefully, my son. If he wears a worried countenance, he is an American fighting for business. If he wears a gas mask, you will know he is a European fighting to live. Listen carefully—and if you hear him speak out boldly, unafraid, a free man, you will know he is an American. If you hear him speak in a bated whisper, fearful, turning his head left and right to see if he is being overheard, you can be absolutely certain of one thing—he is not an American.

Walk into homes, my son, and if you find food and comfort and hear echoes of laughter and young people speaking of their dreams of tomorrow, you will know they can be Americans. If you find tables bare of food and warehouses loaded down by supplies stored for war, if you find children who no longer dream but count each tomorrow as one more day towards a new devastation, you will know you are in an old, weary world, my son.

Walk into schools and universities—and if you find teachers who are free to teach and pupils who are free to inquire, you will know you are very likely in America, for there you will find the sons and daughters of all men, all free to learn and to speak regardless of race or religion. But if you find rigid regimentation, and you find schools are barred to some, and open to some, and only what one man believes to be true is taught, you will know by the heads which are bent down and the eyes from which all spark and love of life and living are gone—you will know you are in an old world, my son.

Do you find men who worship God as they believe in their hearts? Do you find men free to speak out, to write and to read and feel no terror? You will know you are in America, or in one of the few remaining countries where such freedom still lives, my son. . . .

Go into legislative assemblies. Do you hear a man stand up to protest and declare his political opposition? Do you hear debate which is free? Do you hear men vote and say, 'No, I vote no,' even when majorities say 'Yes'? Do you hear men rule in courts of law and say, 'This law which you have passed is illegal because it violates our constitution, our bill of rights, and our sacred concept of freedom'? If you do, you may know that that is the American way, my son. But if you find men waiting for one man to say what tomorrow shall bring, . . . then you will know that you are in a dying world, my son, where few men are free. . . . You will know you are in a world, my son, where life is a strange interlude between wars—between generations which are born only to die in pain and travail and mud. Realizing all this, my son, you will say in the quiet of your heart, as many millions of Americans are saying . . .

"Thank God for America."

THE IDEALS OF EASTER AND SPRING

Drawing by John Walter, IDEALS CHRISTMAS 1963
Painting opposite by George Hinke
Cover, IDEALS EASTER 1947

The springtime of the year has always been a time to celebrate the reawakening of nature and a time to renew our own faith. By springtime of 1946, when the first Easter issue of *Ideals* arrived in American homes, war was over, and the often-difficult business of rebuilding lives was begun. In the pages of that Easter issue were words celebrating the miracle of spring and the miracle of Christ's rebirth, words that lifted the spirits of Americans fresh from the terrible ordeal of war and reminded us of the wonderful and infinite power of faith. Today, *Easter Ideals* has become, for many American families, a part of the ritual of spring, its arrival in the mailbox as dependable as the first green shoots of the crocus peeking up through the snow.

EASTER
ideals

Up Pops Spring

Esther Kem Thomas

IDEALS EASTER 1947
Drawing by John Walter, IDEALS MOTHER'S DAY 1966

The old sun took the earth one day
    And turned it inside out.
Its dormant possibilities
    I knew without a doubt,
But during winter's ice-bound spell
    Each year my eyes forget
The magic of a blade of grass
    And purple violet . . .
Until one day a spell is cast
    That makes my pulses sing—
The season waves a magic wand,
    And up pops spring!

The river bounds and pounds itself
    Among the willow roots;
The sucking soil yields to the weight
    Of muddied rubber boots;
The corners of the fenced-in fields
    Are melted out foursquare;
The horse-trough floats its icy boats,
    And earth scents fill the air;
The handle on the barnyard pump
    Has lost its sticker cling—
The last of winter drips away,
    And up pops spring!

Nothing Like Spring

Adam N. Reiter
IDEALS SPRING 1949

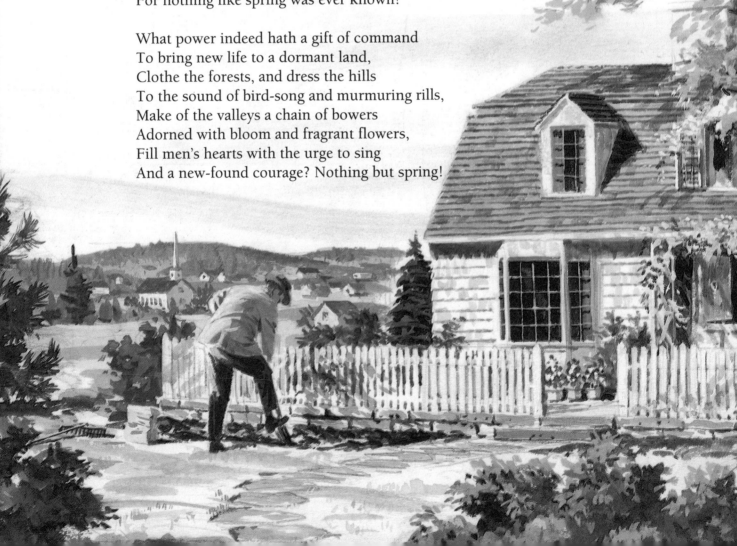

There's many a beautiful sight to see
And many a wonderful place to be,
Many a splendid deed to do,
That cheers a man as he battles through;
There's many a worthy need to fill
That lends a smile, or a transient thrill;
But nothing in this old world can bring
The surge of joy that comes with spring!

What man-made music can match the note
That wells from a robin's merry throat?
What art or craft can change the scene
From desolate brown to shimmering green,
Or call the violets forth at will,
Or paint the face of a daffodil?
'Tis a thing sublime that stands alone,
For nothing like spring was ever known!

What power indeed hath a gift of command
To bring new life to a dormant land,
Clothe the forests, and dress the hills
To the sound of bird-song and murmuring rills,
Make of the valleys a chain of bowers
Adorned with bloom and fragrant flowers,
Fill men's hearts with the urge to sing
And a new-found courage? Nothing but spring!

Spring
ideals

The Believers

Elizabeth York Case

IDEALS SPRING 1949
Painting from WORDS OF COMFORT 1968
Painting opposite by GEORGE HINKE
Cover, IDEALS SPRING 1949

There is no unbelief;
Whoever plants a seed beneath the sod
And waits to see it push away the clod,
He trusts in God.

Whoever says, when clouds are in the sky,
"Be patient, heart, light breaketh by and by,"
Trusts the Most High.

Whoever sees 'neath winter's fields of snow
The silent harvest of the future grow,
God's power must know.

The heart that looks on when eyelids close
And dares to live his life in spite of woes,
God's comfort knows.

There is no unbelief;
And day by day, and night, unconsciously
The heart lives by the faith the lips deny;
God knoweth why.

HE PASSED THIS WAY

Letitia Morse Nash

IDEALS EASTER 1947
Drawing by Ray App, IDEALS EASTER 1967

He passed this way, and sleeping Earth
Springs into life beneath His feet;
The seeds and bulbs that dormant lay
Send forth a message, green and sweet.
The hard bare trees that for long months
Gave not a sign of growth or life
Burst into leaf and blossom fair,
And all the Earth with joy is rife.
Tall Easter lilies, white and fair,
Proclaim the triumph of our King.
He passed this way, and all the Earth
Shall joyously His praises sing.

He passed this way, and stumbling feet
Walk straight and sure because He came.
And hands that faltered at their task
Are blessed and strengthened in His name.
He makes the groping blind to see,
The deaf to hear, the blind to speak,
And brings a blessing of sweet peace
To troubled ones that comfort seek.
He heals the broken hearts of men
And does their haunting fears allay.
And Earth may hope this Eastertime
Because our Saviour passed this way.

 hen cometh Jesus with them unto a place called Gethsemane, and saith unto the disciples, Sit ye here, while I go and pray yonder. And he took with him Peter and the two sons of Zebedee, and began to be sorrowful and very heavy. Then saith he unto them, My soul is exceeding sorrowful, even unto death: tarry ye here, and watch with me. And he went a little farther, and fell on his face, and prayed, saying, O my Father, if it be possible, let this cup pass from me: nevertheless not as I will, but as thou wilt. And he cometh unto the disciples, and findeth them asleep, and saith unto Peter, What, could ye not watch with me one hour? Watch and pray, that ye enter not into temptation: the spirit indeed is willing, but the flesh is weak. He went away again the second time, and prayed, saying, O my Father, if this cup may not pass away from me, except I drink it, thy will be done.

Matthew 26: 36-42

Painting opposite by Ken Gunall, EASTER GREETINGS 1966

One Solitary Life

Author Unknown

IDEALS CHRISTMAS 1944
Painting opposite by George Hinke, IDEALS CHRISTMAS 1944

Here is a man who was born in an obscure village, the child of a
peasant woman. He grew up in another obscure village. He worked
in a carpenter shop until He was thirty, and then for three years He
was an itinerant preacher. He never wrote a book.
He never held an office.

He never owned a home. He never set foot inside a big city. He
never travelled two hundred miles from the place where He was
born. He had no credentials but Himself.

He had nothing to do with this world except the naked power of His
divine manhood. While still a young man, the tide of popular opinion
turned against Him. His friends ran away. One of them denied Him.
He was turned over to his enemies. He went through the mockery of
a trial. He was nailed upon a cross between two thieves.

His executioners gambled for the only piece of property he had on
earth when He was dying, and that was His coat. When He was dead,
He was taken down and laid in a borrowed grave through
the pity of a friend.

Nineteen wide centuries have come and gone and today He is the
centerpiece of the human race and the leader of progress.
I am far within the mark when I say that all the armies that
ever marched and all the navies that ever were built,
and all the parliaments that ever sat, and all the kings that ever
reigned, put together have not affected the life of man
upon this earth as powerfully as that One Solitary Life.

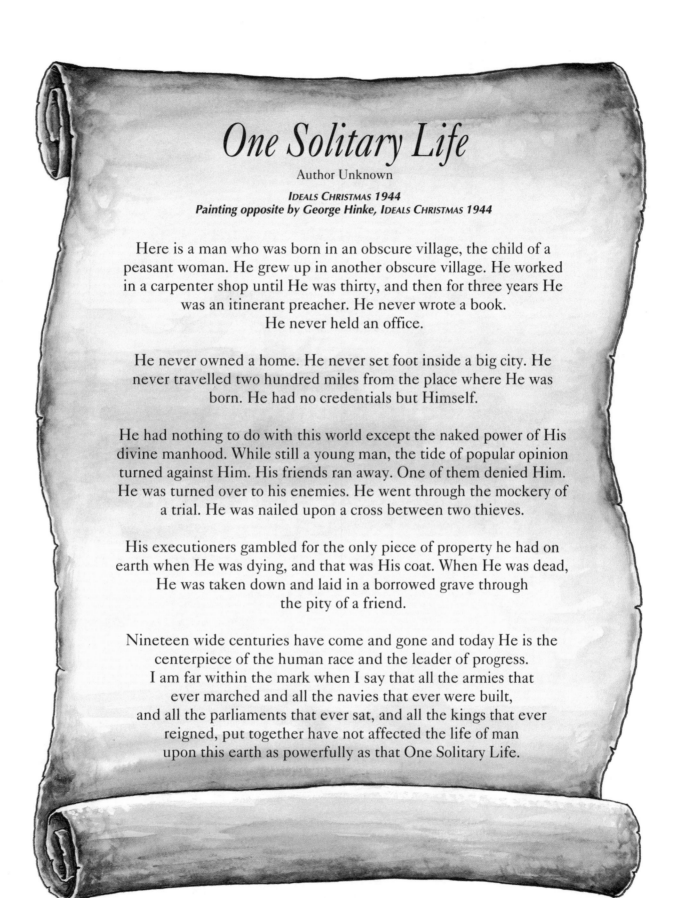

The world is full of mysteries and puzzles on every hand. So many things we do not know and cannot understand. There is much we must accept in Faith as daily living proves. Beyond our veiled and earth-bound mind the Lord Creator moves. He knows the answer to it all, and if our faith is true He will sustain and carry us until each task is through.

Curt A. Mundstock

Engrossment by Curt Mundstock ESPECIALLY FOR MOTHER 1965
Painting opposite by George Hinke, Cover, IDEALS EASTER 1953

Easter
ISSUE

ideals

Geo. Hinke

THE IDEALS OF HOME AND FAMILY

Drawing by Donald Mills, IDEALS COUNTRY 1967
Painting opposite by George Hinke
Cover, IDEALS MOTHER'S 1948

The heart of America has always been—will always be—her families, and the third issue of *Ideals* magazine was devoted to the heart of each and every one of those families: Mother. *Mother's Ideals* appeared for the first time in the spring of 1945, and thereafter *Ideals Mother's Day* became a yearly fixture. The remainder of the family was not neglected, however; through the years there have been issues devoted to fathers, children, and the home. Each has celebrated a different aspect of family life, and each has been treasured by readers who know that no matter how much the times change, we can always find happiness, comfort, love, and stability in the embrace of our families.

Mother's ideals

Mothers

Author Unknown
MOTHER'S IDEALS 1948

I think God took the fragrance of a flower,
A pure white flower, which blooms not for world praise
But which makes sweet and beautiful some bower;
The compassion of the dew, which gently lays
Reviving freshness on the fainting earth
And gives to all the tired things new birth;
The steadfastness and radiance of stars,
Which lift the soul above confining bars;
The gladness of fair dawns; the sunset's peace;
Contentment which from "trivial rounds" asks no release;
The life which finds its greatest joy in deeds of love for others—
I think God took these precious things and made of them our mothers.

Drawing by John Slobodnik, IDEALS THANKSGIVING 1976
Photograph opposite by Gerald Koser, IDEALS FRIENDSHIP 1983

My Mother

Author Unknown
MOTHER'S IDEALS 1948

If I were asked to give a thought which in one word would speak
A unity of brotherhood, a sympathy complete,
A hundred happy cheery ways, a mind that knows its own,
Contented midst a throng of folk, yet peaceful when alone,
A heart that sheds its silent glow to brighten many another,
Without a moment of delay, I'd say, "You mean my mother."

No Occupation

Elsie Duncan Yale

IDEALS MOTHER'S 1948
Drawing by Donald Mills, ESPECIALLY FOR MOTHER 1965

She rises up at break of day,
And through her tasks she races;
She cooks the meal as best she may
And scrubs the children's faces;
Schoolbooks, lunches, ribbons, too,
All need consideration,
And yet the census man insists
She has "no occupation."

When breakfast dishes all are done,
She bakes a pudding, maybe;
She cleans the rooms up one by one,
With one eye watching baby;
The mending pile she then attacks
By way of variation,
And yet the census man insists
She has "no occupation."

She irons for a little while,
Then presses pants for Daddy;
She welcomes with a cheery smile
Returning lass and laddie;
A hearty dinner next she cooks
(No time for relaxation),
And yet the census man insists
She has "no occupation."

For lessons that the children learn
The evening scarce is ample;
To "Mother dear" they always turn
For help with each example;
In grammar and geography
She finds her relaxation,
And yet the census man insists
She has "no occupation."

Mother's Job

Edgar A. Guest

IDEALS MOTHER'S 1948

I'm just the man to make things right,
To mend a sleigh or make a kite,
Or wrestle on the floor and play
Those rough and tumble games, but say!
Just let him get an ache or pain,
And start to whimper and complain,
And from my side he'll quickly flee
To clamber on his mother's knee.

I'm good enough to be his horse
And race with him along the course.
I'm just the friend he wants each time
There is a tree he'd like to climb,
And I'm the pal he's eager for
When we approach a candy store;
But for his mother straight he makes
Whene'er his little stomach aches.

He likes, when he is feeling well,
The kind of stories that I tell,
And I'm his comrade and his chum,
And I must march behind his drum.
To me through thick and thin he'll stick,
Unless he happens to be sick.
In which event, with me he's through—
Only his mother then will do.

Little Girls Are Best

Edgar A. Guest

IDEALS CHILDREN'S 1946
Pencil Drawing by Frances Hook, IDEALS EASTER 1971
Pastel opposite by Frances Hook, IDEALS EASTER 1966

Little girls are mighty nice.
Take' em any way they come;
They are always worth their price;
Life without 'em would be glum.
Run earth's lists of treasures through;
Pile 'em high until they fall—

Gold an' costly jewels, too:
Little girls are best of all.

Nothing equals 'em on earth!
I'm an old man, an' I know
Any little girl is worth
More than all the gold below;
Eyes o' blue or brown or gray,
Raven hair or golden curls—
There's no joy on earth today
Quite so fine as little girls.

Pudgy nose or freckled face,
Fairy-like or plain to see—
God has surely blessed the place
Where a little girl may be;
They're the jewels of His crown
Dropped to earth from heaven above,
Like wee angels sent down
To remind us of His love.

God has made some lovely things—
Roses red an' skies o' blue,
Trees an' babbling silver springs,
Gardens glistening with dew—
But take every gift to man,
Big an' little, great an' small,
And judge it on its merits, an'
Little girls are best of all!

That Lad of Mine

H. Howard Biggar

IDEALS CHILDREN'S 1946
Drawing by Frances Hook, IDEALS EASTER 1971
Pastel opposite by Frances Hook, IDEALS INSPIRATION 1964

I would not have that lad of mine
Think life is just a quest for fame
And that success is gauged by wealth;
I'd have him know that life's a game,
A battle he may lose or win,
With courage gone, or lifted chin.

I'd have him know that days ahead
Will test his mettle, brawn, and brain;
Throughout the years I'd have him know
That life is joys and tears and pain,
And that a measure of success
Is helping folks to happiness.

I want that lad of mine to play
The game of life with sturdy heart,
In every struggle that he'll meet,
In hamlet, countryside, or mart;
I'd like to have him understand
The friendship of an outstretched hand.

I want that lad of mine to have
The time to give a word of cheer
To folks he meets along the way
Whose lives are dark and drab and drear.
I want him always shooting square
And playing hard and clean and fair.

As You Go through Life

Ella Wheeler Wilcox

IDEALS CHILDREN'S 1946
Drawing by Charles Ropp, VALENTINE GREETINGS 1965
Photograph opposite by Ralph Luedtke

Don't look for the flaws as you go through life;
And even when you find them,
It is wise and kind to be somewhat blind
And look for the virtue behind them,
For the cloudiest night has a hint of light
Somewhere in its shadows hiding.
It is better by far to hunt for a star
Than the spots on the sun abiding.

The current of life runs ever away
To the bosom of God's great ocean.
Don't set your force 'gainst the river's course
And think to alter its motion.

Don't waste a curse on the universe—
Remember it lived before you.
Don't butt at the storm with your puny form
But bend and let it go o'er you.

This world will never adjust itself
To suit your whims to the letter;
Some things must go wrong your whole life long,
And the sooner you know it the better.
It is folly to fight with the Infinite
And go under at last on a wrestle.
The wiser man shapes into God's plan
As the water shapes into a vessel.

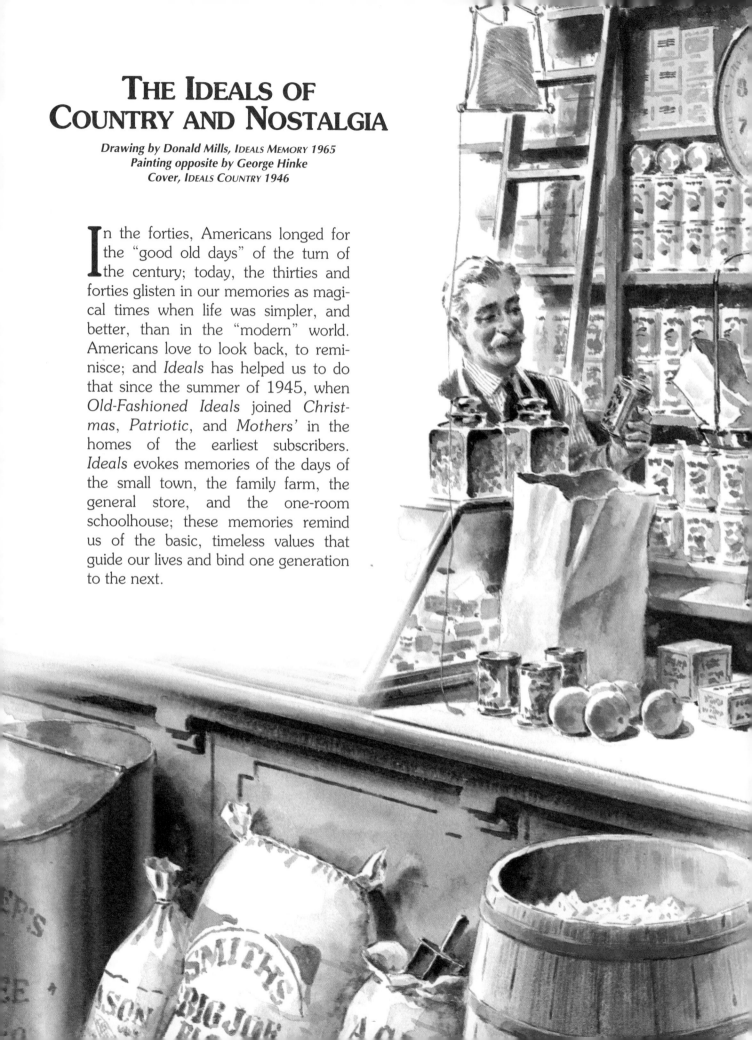

THE IDEALS OF COUNTRY AND NOSTALGIA

Drawing by Donald Mills, IDEALS MEMORY 1965
Painting opposite by George Hinke
Cover, IDEALS COUNTRY 1946

In the forties, Americans longed for the "good old days" of the turn of the century; today, the thirties and forties glisten in our memories as magical times when life was simpler, and better, than in the "modern" world. Americans love to look back, to reminisce; and *Ideals* has helped us to do that since the summer of 1945, when *Old-Fashioned Ideals* joined *Christmas*, *Patriotic*, and *Mothers'* in the homes of the earliest subscribers. *Ideals* evokes memories of the days of the small town, the family farm, the general store, and the one-room schoolhouse; these memories remind us of the basic, timeless values that guide our lives and bind one generation to the next.

ideals
COUNTRY

On a High Green Hill

Grace Noll Crowell

IDEALS COUNTRY 1946
Photograph by Darwin Van Campen, IDEALS EASTER 1964

I shall walk today upon a high green hill;
I shall forget the walls and the roofs of the town;
This burden, strapped to my back, shall be unloosed,
And I shall leave it there when I come down.

Warm is the hill upon which I shall walk today;
Gold is the sun upon the close-cropped grass,
And something of the peace of grazing sheep
Shall permeate my being as I pass.

Something of the look within their eyes,
Of upland pastures and of clean wind blown,
The tranquil, trusting look of those who know
A shepherd watches, I shall make my own.

And I shall gather the little wind flowers there
And press their sweetness upon my heart to stay;
Then I shall go back to the walls and the roofs of the town,
Stronger than I have been for many a day.

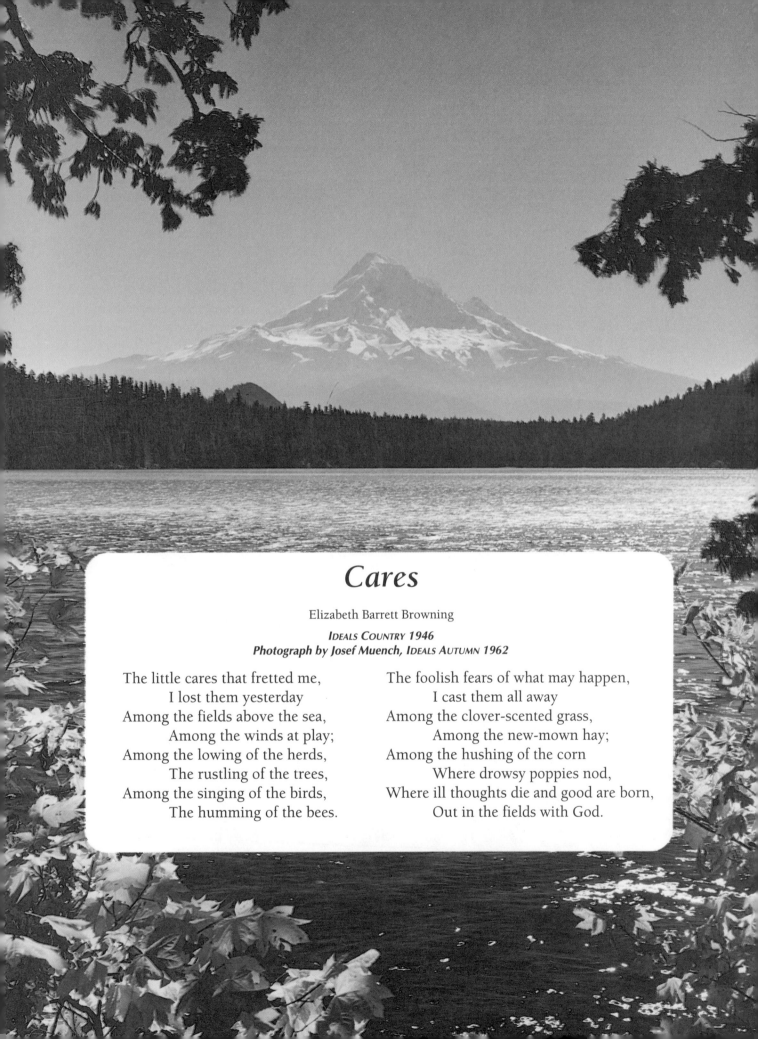

Cares

Elizabeth Barrett Browning

IDEALS COUNTRY 1946
Photograph by Josef Muench, IDEALS AUTUMN 1962

The little cares that fretted me,
    I lost them yesterday
Among the fields above the sea,
    Among the winds at play;
Among the lowing of the herds,
    The rustling of the trees,
Among the singing of the birds,
    The humming of the bees.

The foolish fears of what may happen,
    I cast them all away
Among the clover-scented grass,
    Among the new-mown hay;
Among the hushing of the corn
    Where drowsy poppies nod,
Where ill thoughts die and good are born,
    Out in the fields with God.

Old-Fashioned Stuff

Edgar A. Guest

IDEALS OLD-FASHIONED 1945
Drawing by Donald Mills, *IDEALS HOME* 1965

My father was very old-fashioned, they
said,
With notions long passed out of date.
He fancied the best way of getting ahead
Was to work and have patience to wait.
By practice, he told us, skill came to the
hand;
From study comes learning, he'd say,
And it grieved him to think that the
youth of the land
Could believe in an easier way.

"If it's roses you'd grow you must dig in
the soil;
If you'd rule you must learn to obey.
If money you'd spend you must earn it by
toil."
My father would frequently say,

"If a dollar you borrow, a dollar return.
Debt is something all honest men pay."
And it grieved him to think that his
teachings we'd spurn
Or believe in an easier way.

Well, we've lived and we've laughed
through the wise-cracking age,
And of smartness we've taken our fill;
We are ready, I think, to bring back to
life's stage
Work, honesty, patience, and skill.
The start's at the bottom and not at
the top;
As my old-fashioned father would say,
"The way to the desk is to work in the
shop."
And there's never an easier way.

A Little Town

Author Unknown

Ideals Home 1948

I like to live in a little town,
Where the trees meet over the street;
You wave your hand and say "Hello!"
To every man that you meet.

I like to stop for a minute
Outside of a grocery store
And hear the kindly gossip
Of the folks moving in next door.

For life is interwoven
With friends you learn to know,
And you feel their joys and sorrows
As they daily come and go.

So I'm glad to live in a little town
And care no more to roam;
For every house in a little town
Is more than a house—it's a home!

Days of Long Ago

Frank Carleton Nelson

IDEALS OLD-FASHIONED 1945
Drawing by Cliff Sutherland, IDEALS HOMETOWN 1958
Photograph opposite, IDEALS OLD FASHIONED 1964

Sometimes I get to dreaming of the Days of Long Ago
And in fancy see the faces of the friends I used to know
In the happy days of childhood, when my heart was free from care
And the sun was always shining and the birds were everywhere.
In retrospect I view the scene, and, oh, it seems so good
To live again in memory in that old neighborhood,
Where neighbor lived for neighbor and not for self alone,
For the happiness of others as well as for his own.

Once more I seem to wander up a little narrow lane,
Almost buried out of sight 'twixt fields of yellow grain,
And I come up to a cottage with red roses covered o'er
And behold my dear old Mother, as she stands there in the door
With arms outstretched to greet me and a smile upon her face,
And I hear her say, "God Bless You," as I enter her embrace;
As I live it o'er in fancy, it just somehow seems to me,
'Twas just about the kind of place that heaven's going to be.

But soon the dream is ended, and I waken with a start,
And thoughts of disappointment seem to flow into my heart;
For time has wrought its changes, and the old home's gone today,
And the angels came for Mother, and they bore her soul away.

But it seems I see her waiting, as she did in days of yore,
Waiting now to greet me, up there in Heaven's door;
And it brings a sweeter pleasure for the dawning of that day
When I will lay life's troubles and earthly cares away
And stroll up there and meet her, for she's waiting now, I know,
Waiting, as she used to, in the Days of Long Ago.

The General Store

Strickland Gillilan

IDEALS COUNTRY 1946
Photograph opposite by Ralph Luedtke, IDEALS MEMORY 1965

I'd know it by the sight of it; I'd know it by the smell;
I'd know it by the sound of it, and know it mighty well.
I'd know it if you set me down at midnight 'mid the scent
Of coffee, "coal oil," sugar bins, and country butter blent.
With eyes shut, I can smell again the prints upon the shelf.
Amid the hickory shirting, you could do the same yourself
If you had lived among them in the days when life was bleak
And all you saw was in the town—say every other week.

On that side is the candy—I can see it now, and, oh,
How good those striped sticks used to look in days of long ago!
On this side is the muslin with blue trade marks printed on,
The bleached and unbleached side by side; and here's some simple lawn
And dimity that wouldn't sell (they'd bought it by mistake);
Some blacking, fans, and currycombs, with hoe and garden rake.
We used to carry in the eggs and butter, and we'd buy
Our sugar, tea, and bluing, and the concentrated lye.

We used to wander back into the small room where they kept
The kerosene and axle grease—'twas hardly ever swept;
But there it was we found the scales and weighed ourselves and said
It wasn't like the steelyards out in our old wagon shed.
'Twas there that in the springtime pa would buy us all straw hats,
The ten cent kind made out of straw they use for making mats.
In fall we got our foot gear that must last the winter through,
For pa said: "Them's yer winter boots—ye've got to make 'em do."

I've been in houses mercantile that covered blocks and blocks;
I've seen the clerks that swarm around in bevies and in flocks;
I've seen the elevators; but I cannot make it seem
Like anything substantial, for 'tis nothing but a dream.
To me the real "store" will be, as long as life shall last,
That happy country village place I knew back in the past,
With just one clerk to sell you things, some fellow that you knew,
Though sometimes on a circus day there'd be as high as two.
No fun to do the tradin' like I used to anymore—
But how clear is memory's picture of that general country store!

THE IDEALS OF
AUTUMN AND THANKSGIVING

Drawing by Donald Mills, IDEALS RURAL 1966
Painting opposite by George Hinke
Cover, IDEALS THANKSGIVING 1949

Autumn is a time for reflection, a time for taking stock of our lives and giving thanks for our blessings. When the very first *Ideals Autumn* issue appeared in the fall of 1945, Americans had much to be thankful for. War was over, sons and daughters were returning home, and families were united once more. In the decades of autumns since, *Ideals* has remained a part of the season, celebrating the dazzling natural beauty of the autumn months, expressing the joyous and reflective moods of the holiday, and paying tribute to the uniquely American traditions of Thanksgiving.

Autumn

Marion Doyle

IDEALS THANKSGIVING 1949
Photographs both pages by Ralph Luedtke
IDEALS AUTUMN 1962

If the autumn of life is half as lovely
As the autumn of the earth, I shall not grieve
For the vanished days of the rapturous spring
Nor beg for one moment of reprieve.

I have loved the snows of hawthorn and plum
That rivaled the frost flakes' mystic designs,
But what of a world in crimson and gold
With wild grapes spilling their purple wines!

And if winter shall come? I am content
To leave my life in the hands of God,
Whose mind could conceive the autumn of earth
And star it with asters and goldenrod.

Harvest Time

Harry Aley

IDEALS THANKSGIVING 1949

Now hear the harvest's victorious sound!
O'er all the land great combines fling
Their outstretched arms and garner in
Where faith and seed found friendly ground.

Now smell the fragrance off plain and hill!
Pile up you, your wrested gain.
Unto the good and bad alike it came;
The love of God the Father bodes no ill.

Now weigh thy bread around the festive board!
Be glad of life and of a heart to sing,
For once a serf today you are a King;
O Brother, thine heritage is of the Lord!

Harvest Hymn

John Greenleaf Whittier

IDEALS THANKSGIVING 1949
DRAWING BY DONALD MILLS, IDEALS AUTUMN REFLECTION 1974
Painting opposite by Francis Chase, IDEALS THANKSGIVING 1968

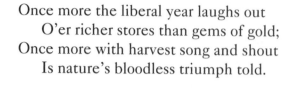

Once more the liberal year laughs out
    O'er richer stores than gems of gold;
Once more with harvest song and shout
    Is nature's bloodless triumph told.

Our common mother rests and sings
    Like Ruth among her garnered sheaves;
Her lap is full of goodly things;
    Her brow is bright with autumn leaves.

Oh, favors old, yet ever new;
    Oh, blessings with the sunshine sent!
The bounty overruns our due;
    The fullness shames our discontent.

We shut our eyes; the flowers bloom on;
    We murmur, but the corn ears fill;
We choose the shadow, but the sun
    That casts it shines behind us still

And gives us, with our rugged soil,
    The power to make it Eden fair,
And richer fruits to crown our toil
    Than summer-wedded islands bear.

Who murmurs at his lot today?
    Who scorns his native fruit and bloom
Or sighs for dainties far away,
    Besides the bounteous board of home?

Thank heaven, instead, that freedom's arm
    Can change a rocky soil to gold,
That brave and generous lives can warm
    A climb with northern ices cold.

And let these altars, wreathed with flowers
    And piled with fruits, awake again
Thanksgivings for the golden hours,
    The early and the latter rain.

When ye have gathered in the fruit of the land, ye shall keep a feast unto the Lord—and ye shall rejoice before the Lord your God seven days.

Leviticus

Heap high the farmer's wintry hoard!
Heap high the golden corn!
No richer gift has autumn poured
From out her lavish horn.

John Greenleaf Whittier

Remember that what you possess in the world will be found at the day of your death to belong to someone else; but what you are will be yours forever.

Henry van Dyke

Pay as little attention to discouragement as possible. Plough ahead as a steamer does, rough or smooth, rain or shine. To carry your cargo and make your port is the point.

M. Babcock

Enthusiasm is the greatest asset in the world. It overwhelms and engulfs all obstacles. It is nothing more nor less than faith in action.

Henry Chester

If you have not often felt the joy of doing a kind act, you have neglected much and, most of all, yourself.

A. Nielen

The very essence of happiness is honesty, sincerity, and truthfulness. He who would have true happiness for his companion must be clean, straightforward, and sincere. The moment he departs from the right, she will take wings and fly away again.

O. S. Marden

So many Gods, so many creeds, so many paths that wind and wind, when just the art of being kind is all this sad world really needs.

Ella Wheeler Wilcox

There never was a person who did anything worth doing who did not receive more than he gave.

Henry Ward Beecher

America is another name for opportunity. Our whole history appears like a last effort of divine providence on behalf of the human race.

Ralph Waldo Emerson

Drawing by Donald Mills, IDEALS THANKSGIVING 1964

Thanksgiving

Henry C. Churchman

IDEALS THANKSGIVING 1949
Drawing by Cliff Sutherland, IDEALS EASTER 1953
Photograph opposite by Gerald Koser, IDEALS THANKSGIVING 1983

I thank Thee, God, with grateful heart, today,
For all those blessings Thou hast brought my way.
What though of worldly goods my store is less
Than neighbors on my left and right possess;
What though no fields of golden grain are mine,
No flock of sheep nor herds of lowing kine;
What though no precious gems my coffers hold,
No heaps of minted silver nor of gold?
For all this wondrous wealth cannot control
Or buy the wealth of gladness in a soul.

The sun, in all its glory, God, is mine,
The scents the breezes waft me from the pine,
The thrush that sings beneath the hazel hedge,
The river lapping at its pebbled edge.
Mine is the grandeur of the sky at night,
The untold stars that conjure my delight,
The path that leads me through the wooded dell,
The kindly hearts that know my wants so well.
And so, O God, with grateful heart I say,
I thank Thee for Thy blessed gifts today.

He ain't heavy, Mister — He's m' brother.

Drawing by Cliff Sutherland, IDEALS CHRISTMAS 1944

ACKNOWLEDGMENTS

LITTLE GIRLS ARE BEST from *RHYMES OF CHILDHOOD* by Edgar Guest, copyright ©1924 by The Reilly & Lee Co. MOTHER'S JOB from *THE PATH TO HOME* by Edgar Guest, copyright ©1919 by The Reilly & Lee Co. SLEIGH BELLS from *ALL IN A LIFETIME* by Edgar Guest, copyright ©1938 by The Reilly & Lee Co. Used by permission of the author's estate. LET US KEEP CHRISTMAS, A MOTHER TO HER SON IN SERVICE, and ON A HIGH GREEN HILL from *APPLES OF GOLD*. Copyright ©1950 by HarperCollins and *SOME BRIGHTER DAWN* by Grace Noll Crowell. Copyright ©1943 by HarperCollins. Reprinted by arrangement with Harper San Francisco, a division of Harper Collins Publishers. Our sincere thanks to the following authors whom we were unable to contact: Harry Aley for HARVEST TIME; H. Howard Biggar for THAT LAD OF MINE; Henry C. Churchman for THANKSGIVING; Marion Doyle for AUTUMN; Strickland Gillilan for THE GENERAL STORE; R. Armistead Grady for IS THERE A SANTA CLAUS?; Letitia Morse Nash for HE PASSED THIS WAY; Frank Carleton Nelson for CHRISTMAS DAYS OF LONG AGO and THE DAYS OF LONG AGO; Wilbur B. Nesbit for YOUR FLAG AND MY FLAG; Esther Cushman Randall for BELLS OF EASTER; Adam N. Reiter for NOTHING LIKE SPRING; Pliny A. Wiley for THE CHIMES OF CHRISTMAS; and Elsie Duncan Yale for NO OCCUPATION.